Shopping with Dad

Written by
Stephen Rickard

Illustrated by
Helen Stanton

Aran went shopping with Dad.

"Can you get some milk?"
said Dad.
Aran picked up some milk.
He put it in the basket.

"We need some bread. Can you get some bread?" said Dad.
Aran picked up some bread.
He put it in the basket.

"I will get some cheese,"
said Dad.
Dad picked up some cheese
and he put it in the basket.

"Can you get some juice?" said Dad.
Aran picked up some juice and he put it in the basket.

"We need some apples," said Aran.
"Can you get some apples, Dad?"

The basket was full.
"We need to pay,"
said Dad.

"You can pay," said Aran.
"I am too tired.
Too much shopping for me."

milk   bread   cheese

juice   apples